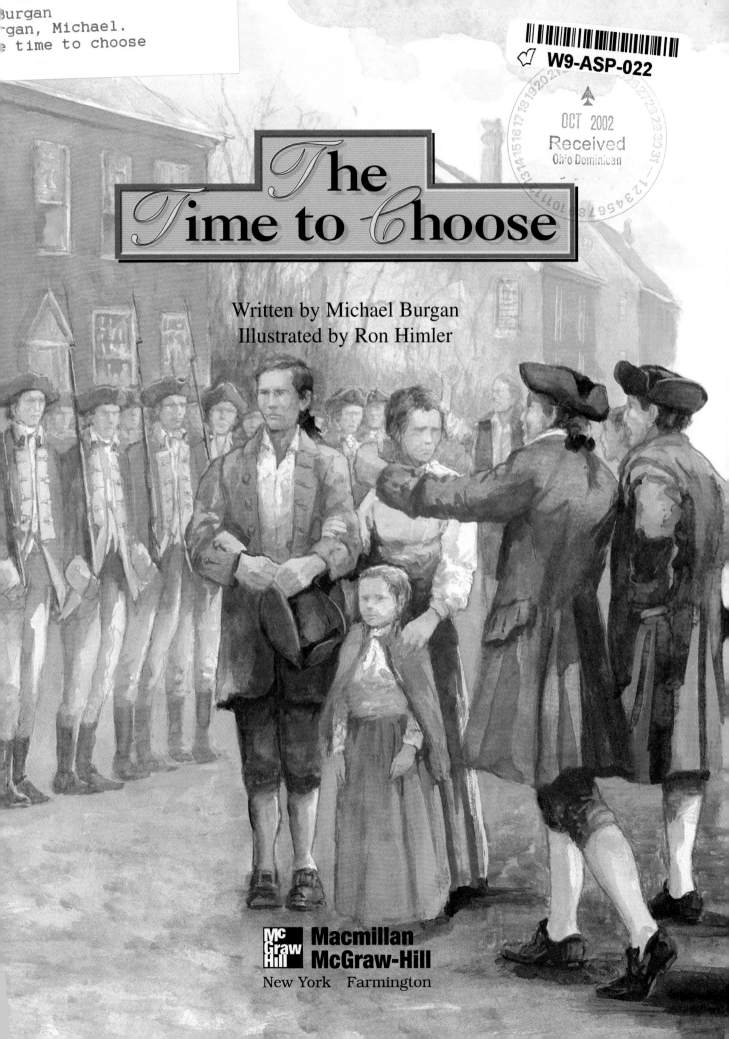

The Time to Choose

Written by Michael Burgan
Illustrated by Ron Himler

Mc Graw Hill **Macmillan McGraw-Hill**

New York   Farmington

July 5, 1769

Today is my birthday. My name is Rebecca White, and I am now ten years old. For a present, Mamma has given me this diary. In it, I will write all that I think, do, and see. I already have a lot to write, as yesterday was filled with excitement.

The lobsters have left Boston! Oh, I know this must sound funny. I don't mean the fish, of course. I mean the British soldiers who landed here almost a year ago. The boys here call them lobsterbacks or lobsters, because of their bright red coats. Mamma would scold me if she knew I used that word. She says we should treat the soldiers with respect. But many people here don't share Mamma's view.

It seems so long ago that the British ships sailed into our harbor. My friend Sally Cooper and I watched the soldiers as they marched along the Long Wharf and up King Street. Some local men cried, "Go back to England!" But the soldiers just kept pouring off the ships.

❖

Later that day, I asked my father why the soldiers had come to Boston.

"They're here to protect the customs officials who collect taxes for the British king," he said. "Some of our neighbors don't like paying taxes to these men. People have been getting angry—even violent. The customs officials fear for their lives."

"Are they afraid of the Patriots?" I asked.

"Where did you hear of them?" Mamma quickly asked.

"Oh, the boys on the street talk of them. They say the Patriots want to protect our freedom."

My father scowled a bit. "Perhaps. But we still have plenty of freedom. We're still citizens of England. I think we should obey the king's laws—unless they are *too* harsh."

Ever since the soldiers arrived, I have heard people talk about liberty, freedom, rights. Many people believe King George III has no right to tax the American colonists. These people certainly don't like British soldiers drilling in our fields and walking through our streets.

But yesterday, the soldiers left. Well, not all of them, but many. I ran to the Long Wharf to watch them leave. The crowd cheered as the men boarded the boats. "Good-bye, lobsters," some shouted. "Enjoy your sail home!"

Later, I told my parents what I'd seen.

"You be careful when you're in the crowds, Rebecca," Mamma warned. "You don't know when trouble might happen."

"But the people were happy, Mamma," I said. "Why would there be trouble?"

"They're happy now," Father said, "but how long will they remain so? British troops are still here. I don't think some people will be happy until the last one leaves."

The day is cool and gray. The trees in the commons are already bare. Father says winter could be early this year, and harsh as well. After school, I helped Mamma spin yarn, then sat with her as she did needlepoint. I tried to be cheery, but I had been troubled since school. Mamma, as always, knew something was wrong.

"Rebecca, you have barely said three words today. What's the matter?"

I bit my lip before speaking. "Mamma, are we Tories?"

Mamma's eyes widened.

"Will Caldwell says everyone who wants freedom is a Patriot, and anyone who doesn't support the Patriots is a Tory. He asked if Father is a Patriot and I said no."

I gulped, then continued my story.

"'So you're a lobster-lover, eh?' he sneered at me. 'You think the king can end our freedom. You're a no-good Tory, Rebecca White!' He sounded so mean, I almost started crying."

Mamma put down her needlepoint. "We are not Tories or Patriots. We have not taken sides. Your father has too much sense to get involved in all this squabbling."

But Father knew what was happening. The city had not calmed since July. Father's customers often talk to him about the troubles. Just yesterday, in Father's barrel shop, I heard him speaking with Mr. Greenwood.

"Some folks threw a few rocks near the guard house last week," Mr. Greenwood said. "Two redcoats were left bleeding."

"The soldiers will strike back sometime," Father said sadly. "Then another gang of Patriots will start more trouble, and things will get worse. I fear how all this will end."

"I just hope I can keep young Sam out of trouble," said Mr. Greenwood. "He's a good lad, but so many of the young men are swept up with cries of 'Liberty, liberty!'"

Sam Maverick works for Mr. Greenwood. I've seen Sam walking along Milk Street. I wonder if he is a Patriot. He seems like a quiet boy, not someone who would start a fight.

When Father came in for supper, I could tell he was still thinking about the gangs and the soldiers. The weather may not be the only thing harsh about this winter.

I don't think I've ever seen a sadder day in my life. Tears still stream down my face and dot this page. Mamma, Father, and I just returned from a funeral. One of my schoolmates, Chris Snider, is dead. A boy just barely older than me, and he was killed in such a ruthless way! Here is what happened, as best as I can tell.

A few days ago, Chris and some other boys were in Dock Square. Mr. Richardson was also there. Mr. Richardson is a Tory, and everyone says he spies for the English. He is a most hated man.

That morning, Mr. Richardson angered the boys out on the street. They began throwing rocks and mud at him. It was a mean thing for them to do, but what Mr. Richardson did next was truly horrible. He ran into his shop, shouting at the boys. Then he pointed his rifle out the window!

"Go off, go off!" he shouted. "I'll fire if you don't stop."

But the boys kept throwing rocks. Mr. Richardson fired, then reloaded and fired again. When the shooting stopped, poor Chris was lying in the street. Blood ran from his stomach. Dr. Warren was called, but it was too late—Chris Snider was dead.

Oh, how the people in the street raged at Richardson! Some wanted to hang him on the spot. Somehow, a Patriot calmed the crowd, and Mr. Richardson was arrested.

Today, it seemed like all of Boston came out to bury Chris. Snow fell as we walked along Newbury Street. Something stirred in my stomach, as if I had heard a scary noise in the middle of the night. I told Father how I felt.

"It's sadness that makes you feel that way, Rebecca. Sadness and fear. I feel it too."

"What are you afraid of, Father?" I asked.

"This killing of Chris Snider was a terrible thing. People are angrier than ever. I don't know if the Patriots can control them."

"What do you mean?"

"I mean, Rebecca, I think there will be more killing. And that will be an even sadder day for all of us."

March 3, 1770

The whole town buzzes today with news of the fight. Yesterday on the docks, some soldiers and ropemakers battled in the street. Sarah Cooper's brother, Jacob, works down there, and he told everyone on the street what he saw.

"It began with just one or two workers knocking about a British soldier. Then the soldier came back with eight or nine more lobsters. But our boys beat them again. Finally, about 40 or so redcoats charged in, carrying clubs and sticks. The workers had weapons too, and they drove the soldiers back to their barracks. What a fight it was!"

"I heard many of the soldiers left with bloodied noses and black eyes," Mamma said.

"It's true, as far as I could tell. They know now the feel of a New England fist," Jacob said, shaking his own.

"You're a Patriot, Jacob?" Father asked.

"Yes sir, I am. We don't need the lobsterbacks parading through our streets, or the king's men telling us how to live." Jacob stopped and eyed my father. "You don't want the English here, do you, Mr. White?"

"I'm no Tory, if that's what you mean. I just don't want any more trouble."

Later, Father told Mamma and me he had already heard more trouble might be at hand. After yesterday's fight, the soldiers were said to have sharpened their swords. They swore revenge against the workers. The Patriots, too, are ready to fight again. Some of the boys say that come Monday, if we hear the bells ringing in the churches, we'll know another battle has begun.

It's almost midnight, later than I've ever stayed up before. But tonight has not been an ordinary night. The soldiers have killed three men on King Street! Two more citizens are close to death, including Mr. Greenwood's helper, Sam Maverick. Chris Snider's death had filled everyone's eyes with tears. But this massacre, as the people already call it, has filled hearts with deep hatred for the British.

After the fights at the docks, the whole city was tense. By bedtime, nothing had happened, though a neighbor did come by and say there had been trouble by the soldiers' barracks. Then, around nine, a bell began to ring at the Brick Meetinghouse. Usually, such ringing means only one thing.

"Fire?" Mamma asked, worried.

"Sounds like it," Father said. He grabbed a leather bucket and headed for the door. Suddenly, more bells began ringing. Father opened the door, and we saw people running by. I heard bits of what they said.

"... lobsterbacks!"

"... a fight ..."

"... pushed the boy into the street!"

"It's worse than a fire," Father said. "I fear it's a riot. The Patriots and the soldiers are going to fight again." Father joined the running crowd.

"I'm coming too," Mamma said.

I jumped out of bed, ready to go with them.

"Rebecca! You stay here!" Mamma insisted. "The street's no place for you now."

"But Mamma!"

"No!" she shouted, rushing down the street. As soon as she was out of sight, I slipped out the door. Hundreds of people ran on either side of me, shouting angrily about the soldiers. The crowd seemed to push me along, as if I were a piece of wood on an ocean wave.

In a few seconds, I reached the riot. Some British soldiers had their guns pointed at a group of boys and men. The group taunted the soldiers and threw coal and snowballs at them. Someone cried, "Fire, fire if you dare!" The soldiers seemed scared, even though they held guns.

Then, a single shot rang out in the street. Five more "bangs" followed. Five men fell to the ground. People all around me screamed and I gasped. Some folks tried to drag the wounded off the streets. I watched in horror as blood darkened the packed snow.

The street fell quiet for a moment. Then the bells began ringing again. Even more people streamed outside. Some carried clubs. Others held knives. The crowd yelled at the soldiers. But before anyone else could kill or be killed, the soldiers were ordered into their barracks.

"Rebecca! What are you doing out here?"

I had hoped to slip away before the crowd left, but Mamma and Father now stood above me. I shook, fearing the punishment I was sure to get. But instead of scolding me, Father picked me up in his broad arms.

"No child should have to see such a massacre," he said. He held me tightly.

"It was terrible, Father!"

"I know, I know," he said quietly.

❖

"What's going to happen now?" I asked as he carried me back to the house.

"I don't know. The people will not stand for this bloodshed. The soldiers must go—all of them."

"And what about you, Father?" I looked into his eyes.

"What do you mean, Rebecca?"

"Are you still not a Patriot and not a Tory? Are you still not involved?"

"Rebecca, I have just seen five unarmed men struck by bullets. One of them, poor Sam, is just a young man who has never harmed a soul. Something is wrong here in Boston, in New England. The king's men have gone too far. Rebecca, from this moment on, I—no, *we* are Patriots. We must stand for freedom and justice, and against this brutal violence."

Mamma nodded sadly in agreement.

When we got home, Father put me to bed, but I couldn't sleep. I got up to write all this down. I have seen and heard so much these past months. I now know Father is right. We are Patriots, and we have chosen the right side. No one who loves liberty will be happy until the British are gone for good.